Where's Peter?

by
EDITH KUNHARDT

Greenwillow Books 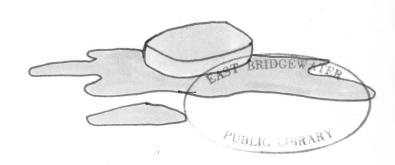 New York

Library of Congress Cataloging-in-Publication Data

Kunhardt, Edith.   Where's Peter?
Summary: Peter pretends to be invisible in the
bathtub, a game he shares with his baby sister
Abby when she becomes old enough for the big tub.
[1. Baths—Fiction.   2. Babies—Fiction.
3. Brothers and sisters—Fiction]   I. Title.
PZ7.K94905Wh   1988   [E]   86-27061
ISBN 0-688-07204-6   ISBN 0-688-07205-4 (lib. bdg.)

OcT 1988

To Peter Whiting Kunhardt, Jr.

Every night Peter was invisible.
Every time he took off his clothes, climbed
into his bath, and put a washcloth on his
back, he became invisible.

"Where's Peter?" asked his mother.
She looked in the bath water.
She looked under the sink.

She looked in the closet.
"He's all gone," she said.

"Where's Peter?" asked Peter's father.
He looked in the medicine cabinet.
He looked behind the chair.

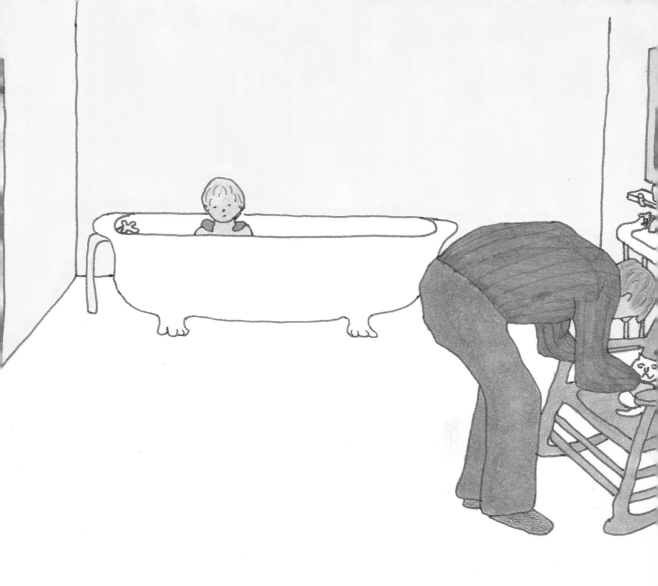

He looked under the cat.

"He's all gone," Peter's father said.

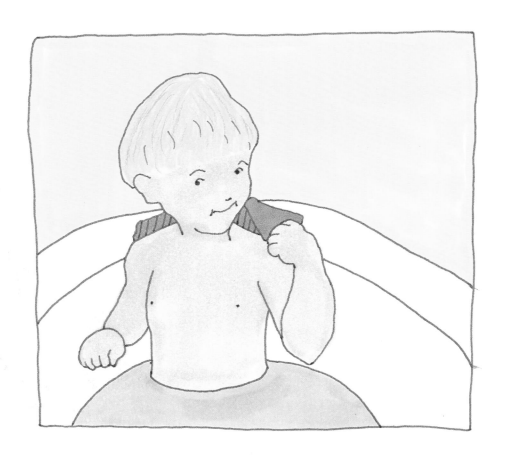

Every night Peter became visible again.
"Here I am," he said, pulling the
washcloth off his back.

"There you are!" said his mother,
   clapping her hands.
"There you are!" said his father,
   smiling a big smile.

Pretty soon Peter's mother had a baby,
so Peter had a baby sister.

When Abby was little,
she took baths in the sink.

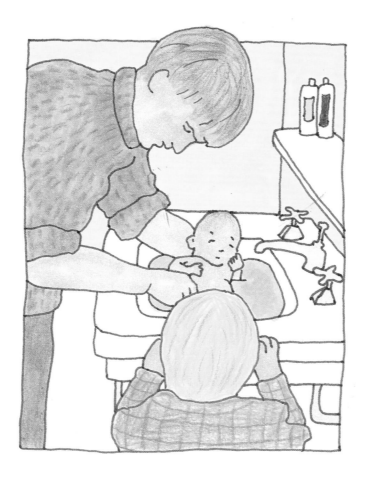

Peter watched his father hold the baby
carefully as he washed her. Peter held her
foot, but she kicked and splashed him.

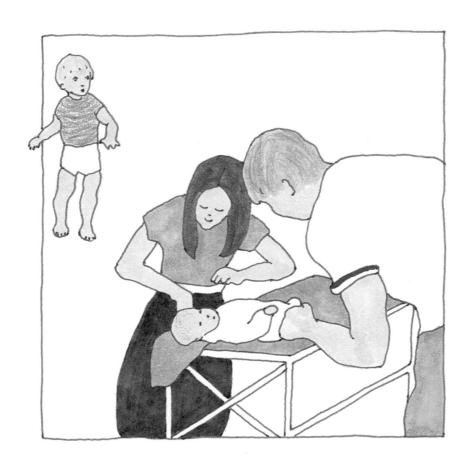

Peter still became invisible, but
not all the time. His parents
were busy with the baby.

Abby grew fast.

Soon she could sit up.

Soon she said her first words.

Soon she took a bath in the big bathtub.

One night Peter put a washcloth
on Abby's back.
"Where's Abby?" he asked.

"Yes, where is she?" asked his
mother. "Look for her, Peter."
Abby wasn't under the sink.

She wasn't in the hamper.
She wasn't behind the tub.

"There you are!" cried Peter, pulling the washcloth off Abby's back.

Peter's mother hugged him tight.

"Now Abby knows your game!" she said.

"And I know you're my best, best boy."

Peter hugged her back. He knew he was.